EROTIC SHORT TALES

EXPLICIT DIRTY EROTICA SHORT STORIES

STEFAN MCKINNIS,CHANEY KEES, DAKOTA
DEECE, BLAINE TELLER,TRINITY
STYLLER,FARRAH SEAGER,HELANA
PARKINS,TRISTA JACO,MACKENZIE
HARNDEN

plicit Press
Erotica Fiction

CHAPTER 1

A WET AND WILD NIGHT TO REMEMBER

THE CLUB OASIS was booming tonight. You could feel the electricity throughout the entire place. Rozlin was glad to see that her business venture in opening the hottest night-club in the San Francisco area was a huge success. Oasis was the number one nightclub for four months in a row now and Rozlin was going to make sure that the club stayed in that spot. She took the time to look at her surroundings and all of the people in the club tonight. There was something about the feeling of success that made her want to have some fun after work tonight. She was highly aroused by all of the dancing, watching all of the bodies grinding up against each other. As she made her way to the back of the club, she started watching from her private room that was not only soundproof but it was also made with one-way glass. That way she could see what was going on and no one knew that she was watching. And she had to admit she loved her room because she could have some fun with Leon during work if she wanted. After all, she had a futon in the room that turned into a bed with one pull.

. . .

Sitting at her desk in her room, she noticed that even as the night continued the club continued to stay busy. By no means was she complaining at all, but she knew that they could not stay open past 1 am because some of her employees would have her neck. After relaxing for a bit she looked up at her clock... 11:oopm "One hour to go," she thought. Now the crowd was starting to thin out the closer they got to midnight.

It was almost closing time as she continued to watch over everything, running as smooth as it was. Taking some time to enjoy the music she went out to the dance floor, dancing with the rest of the people that were still there. After a while, the last of the night's customers walked out the door. Rozlin walked over to the bar where her business partner Leon was wiping down the bar and getting ready to take the cash to her office.

Leaning up against the bar, she smiled at Leon. "How much do you think we made tonight just in the bar? I noticed while I was making my rounds that you never had a dull moment." Laughing, Leon looked up at Rozlin. "You could say that again. I bet the bar alone made $4,000 tonight. However, we are going to have to think about adding Axel as a full-time bartender to help me keep up with the growing crowds."

"Well if you think that bringing Axel full time would be beneficial I think it would be something that we should mention to him tonight while both of you are here. So why don't you and Axel come to my office when you both are done with your work. I have to do the books tonight."

. . .

She grinned seductively, whispering, "And I am restless and could use some sexual attention tonight if you are up for it that is. And maybe you could convince Ax, to join us. You have to admit it would spice things up." Leon laughed, " Yeah, maybe for you."

"Are you jealous and do not want to share for a night? I promise you, I will make it up to you." She looked him over stopping short at his waist licking her lips. She walked away swaying her hips. He had to admit that he loved it when she teased him like that. It meant that she was not only horny but also that she was in a very kinky mood. He loved it when she was like that because that meant anything was possible. The thought of her being in the mood she was in made him imagine taking her from behind in the ass while Axel was underneath her and letting her ride him. Damn, what a night it was going to be. He had a feeling it was going to go all night, but he was not complaining at all because he loved the time he got to be with Roz.

Looking around he saw that Axel was taking the money from admissions to Roz. He knew that if he did not ask him to have a threesome with Roz he was going to walk in that door and find a surprise. "Hey, Ax wait! I want to ask you something, come here for a minute. After we are done working tonight ...Roz and I are uh... going to hang out and have a few drinks. We were wondering if you would like to join us."

. . .

Axel was a well-built man. He stood at 6'5, 280 lbs. With his blonde hair and blue eyes, Leon wondered why he did not have a girlfriend. And Leon could bet that Axel had excellent stamina that could keep up with Roz on nights like tonight, for sure. He just needed to see if he would be willing to have a threesome with them.

"Sure for a bit man, I have to admit I am itching to get down to Teasers tonight. " Leon smiled, "Really?"

He loved that bar where all the waitresses were topless in bikini bottoms. And if you were lucky, you would have two of them to bring you dinner and a show and some of them would leave with you. He had done that a time or two before he and Roz had a work and fuck relationship. It did have its benefits. "Well, the other thing we wanted to know is if you would join us in a threesome. Roz is in a kinky mood and she would love to have you as one of the participants."

"Man, are you jerkin my chain? I would have never guessed that about Roz. I mean she seems so straight-laced and I would have never thought of her as having a kinky side."

Laughing, Leon looked at the shock on his face. "Looks can be deceiving, she is one kinky woman and she always gets what she wants. But in return we are treated well and get what all men want, to be fucked all of the time and by a smoking hot boss. Where is the downfall to that?"

. . .

"Seriously?"

"Yes, I was asked to ask you and when I saw you heading for the door I knew I needed to stop you because I can tell you that behind that door is Roz in her black lace lingerie, with fishnet stockings and black heels. She wears that outfit when she is in the mood. So if you are ready let's go have some fun." Walking over to the private room, Leon knocked.

"Come in." Just as Leon had said, Roz was in black lace lingerie all the way down to the heels.

God, she was sexy sitting on her desk.

"Put the money in the safe men, I have something I need you to do before you leave tonight." She grinned walking over to the futon that was already pulled out for a bed. Putting the money in the safe, the men walked over to the bed. Neither of them could believe how beautiful she looked even after working. Her long red hair was down and she was on the bed on her knees waiting for both of them to join her.

Leon stood in front of her as he stripped. He tilted her chin up and he kissed her. Damn, she tasted sweet. He wanted more. Pulling away from her, he began stroking his cock for a moment, and then he put the pre cum on his finger putting it in her mouth as he watched her suck it off. When she was done sucking the cum off she began to lick the top of his throbbing head a while Axel got up on the bed behind her.

Axel could not believe that this was happening to him as he was sliding his cock in her pussy.

He loved the feel of how tight she was. As he began rocking back and forth, he could hear her moan, but he was taking it slow, as he did not want to hurt her in any way as he was well endowed more than most men were.

After a few minutes, the men switched. Although Leon loved it when she gave him a blowjob, it just did not set right having another man's cock in her tight wet pussy. As he began to pound his cock into her, he felt her pussy clamp down on his cock. "Yeah baby, take it all." Driving his cock further into her he had an idea. What if both men fucked her at the same time? After all, he did want to take her in the ass. This would give him the chance to do that and it would please her even more.

"Baby why don't you ride Axel for a little bit and break him in a little." She grinned, "Are you sure?"
    "Positive."

.   .   .

He knew that if he did not get her to relax his chances of fucking her in the ass were not going to happen. He stood up and walked over to the desk door where there was some oil. Grabbing it, he put some on.

Walking back over he could see that she was relaxed. Coming up behind her, he wrapped his hands in her hair and leaned her forward enough so that he could get his cock in her ass inching carefully. Once he knew he was in then it would be smooth sailing and he would make sure she would come several times before the night was done. This would one wet and wild night to remember for sure for all of them.

Both men worked on her at the same time, listening to her moan and at times scream in ecstasy until she finally did it. "That's it boys, right there, fuck me and fuck me hard," she screamed. She truly did have an insatiable hunger tonight. He had to admit he loved having his cock in her ass because he could always tell when she was about to cum. Her ass would tighten up and she would go still for a moment.

Rozlin looked at Axel. "You are truly built for stamina aren't you? I have come at least 8 times and you have yet to cum." Smiling he put his hands on her hips. "I am gifted, " he said. Smirking, he slowed his pace and then sped up again. Leon could tell that Roz was about to cum again and this time she was going to lose it totally. "Hey Ax, lets both give it to her one more time really good. She is about to cum big time." Both men smiled at one another that her body when on sensory overload as Axel began suckling on her breast and ramming her pussy and Leon began ramming her ass with his cock. Soon after that Roz collapsed, fully sated. That truly was the best night she had had in years and she could guarantee that there would be many more to come.

CHAPTER 2

ENJOYING HER PREGNANCY
A TABOO EROTICA

I RUSHED OVER to the hospital when I found out that my father was hospitalized suddenly with a stroke. There I met my ex-girlfriend Eva. I had not spoken to Eva since our nasty breakup a few months ago. When I discovered that she was pregnant with my child, I found myself wishing that I was a better man. I invited her to my house. We arrived at my house soon after leaving the hospital. Eva's eyes perused the house, smiling. It was familiar territory for her, and I supposed that she was pleased to see that the place was almost untouched; I had made very little changes to the space.

We began chatting about the good times that we'd had here in this very house. "If walls could talk," she chuckled. Her smile was even brighter than I'd ever seen, she was literally glowing. Maybe it had to do with her pregnancy, but I didn't care to understand, I just simply appreciated the fact that she was happy and sharing the warmth of her smile with me.

"I've missed you so much Eva," I seized the opportunity while I was still in her good graces. I pulled her into my arms and planted a soft kiss on her full, lush lips. She kissed me back, her kisses hungry and full of desire. I was pleased with how her body was responding to mine.

Pinning her back against the wall, I began to kiss her even more passionately, my tongue exploring the insides of her mouth. She went wild, her hands roaming freely all over my back. My mouth soon left her lips and trailed downwards to the nape of her neck.

"Oh Josh...I've missed you," she cooed tilting her head to the side, letting out a breath of air.

I worked my way downwards from the nape of her neck to her gorgeous bountiful breasts that were covered by the fabric of her cotton t-shirt. Hoisting the t-shirt up and over her neck, she helped me release her breasts from the constraints of the black lace bra that she wore. Her breasts were huge, and full, almost double their usual size. Her nipples were hard and round, double in size as well.

"Oh, mama..." I whispered with a huge smile on my face as I buried my face into the huge breasts, nibbling at her nipples. Eva moaned out, in ecstasy, as I continued to kiss her nipples, gently lapping my tongue over them, sucking them lightly occasionally.

"I want it now Josh," she moaned her voice filled with desire.

I wanted her now too. I didn't keep her waiting, immediately I unbuckled my pants and dropped everything down to the floor including the boxer shorts that I had on. I gently turned her back towards the wall and parted her legs open I smacked her ass lightly a few times and she moaned and begged me to rid of her leggings and panty, which I did happily, without any sort of resistance. Once completely naked, I stroked my penis a few times, getting it to the degree of hardness that I wanted.

I slipped a finger into her temple of delight. "My gosh, Eva," I groaned. Her pussy was fat and juicy. The thick flesh was warm and inviting, and I bent my head under giving her sweetness a long soft succulent lick.

"Oh baby..." she moaned parting her legs even further. I gave her another long slow lick, taking her clitoris into my mouth at the end of it all. She bucked her pussy onto my mouth as I pleasured her by licking and sucking onto her swollen bud. Her body quivered as tiny spasms rocked through her pussy.

Finally, I pulled my lips away from her core, and replaced it with my massive erection, penetrating the slit of her pussy slowly. A soft moan escaped her lips as I buried my raw meat into her wetness. Pulling out slowly, I penetrated her again this time a little harder. I began moving in rhythm thrusting my dick in and out of her moist core.

The room was filled with her moaning and my panting. Her juices oozed onto my shaft as I lost all control and increased my momentum, ramming her pussy with my cock, over and over. She moaned louder and louder, her pussy bucking against my cock wildly.

Finally, with a mighty thrust and loud groan, we both surrendered our earth-shattering climax.

I exploded a load of my hot semen into her pussy, her juices mixing with mine. It took us a few minutes to calm down from our brief moment of pleasure.

As we walked over to the couch, I could see the swelling of her tummy in front of her. That was my baby in there. A sense of pride mixed with love and care enthralled me and I wanted nothing more than to be with the two of them; Eva and my future son or daughter.

"Marry me," I said to her, without even thinking about it. I was doing the right thing. "Me, marry you? I thought you weren't ready... You like living the single life of a bachelor... remember?" She gave me a serious look.

Pulling her closer to me, I captured her gaze with mine. "I'm not any of these things anymore, I'm Josh – the plumber's son. And that's it...I want you and you alone."

She smiled. I could see the tears welling up in her eyes. "I've waited so long to hear you say that."

"Then say yes...And make me the happiest man alive." "YES! YES! YES!" she yelled with excitement in her voice.

I didn't know what tomorrow holds for us, but I knew that I wanted to be with Eva for the rest of my life. And that was all that mattered to me. At a point in every man's life, he has to make a decision. Do I choose to have a family, or continue sleeping around and risk dying a lonely old man? That was not a risk I wanted to take. Option number one, please. Eva loved me, and I loved her. I wanted nothing more than to raise beautiful babies with her and live a happy life – that probably would have its ups and downs.

CHAPTER 3

INCUBUS

THERE SHE WAS, sound asleep. He had been following her for three nights now. She was an exceptional beauty and would make a great companion for himself. Her skin was almost lucid, it was as pale as his, even though he was the vampire, not her. Her shiny black hair stood in extreme contrast and made her light hazel eyes stand out even more. But now they were closed and Nicholas had plenty of time to admire his sleeping beauty.

Her body was only covered by a short satin nightgown. In her vivid, apparently unpleasant dreams, her legs had fought off the blanket until it spread out on the floor. Her ribcage pushed her breasts up, toward him, in the fast rhythm of her heavy breathing. His radiant deep red eyes fixated on them going up and down.

Oh, how he loved to give her nightmares. She always responded so properly. But even more, he loved his ability to make people do whatever he wanted them to do. He could make them scream, hop like bunnies, or give them the sweetest dreams anyone could think of. With his current favorite toy, the innocent beauty, he loved to scare her. Her body responded in a way that turned him on. Even though he was dead, the sight of her sensual body could fill him with desire.

His mouth opened slightly and revealed two shiny white fangs, as his eyes were glowing with delight. "Be a good girl," he murmured, "and get rid of that annoying piece of fabric. It's just in your way... and in mine."

Unaware of anything, caught in dark dreams before her inner eye, she pulled down the straps of her nightgown, tossing and turning like it were a vicious animal she had to get rid of.

"That's my girl," Nicholas purred. "But let me help you shorten that process."

With his sharp claws, he reached down to her and, using them like a knife, ripped apart her gown. The fabric fell to both her sides and bared her white-as-snow body.

"Oh yes," he approved excitedly, spreading and stiffening his black wings. "That's what I want to see."

His fiery red eyes started to emit a soft light that seemed to soothe her. She stopped tossing and now lay completely still on her back, almost smiling.

"Oh, you like that." Nicholas seemed surprised that the images he was now sending her didn't bother her. Just the opposite, as a matter of fact. She seemed to enjoy the pictures of him making love to her in the most various ways.

Slowly letting her hand slide between her thighs, she sighed.

"How about that?" Nicholas was in awe, getting more and more aroused by the second, just watching her caress her most sensitive spot. A sensual moan escaped her, as her entire body tuned in for pleasure, awaiting more.

Her moaning intensified, her legs spread wider, and

Nicholas could tell she was ready for penetration. His member arose inevitably.

"Is this what you want?" he asked her through her dreams. "Do you want to be fucked by me?" As a response she groaned, still massaging herself sinfully.

"Say it," he demanded.

"Fuck me," she mumbled breathlessly. "Fuck me."

Her words made him grow even harder, and without hesitation, he tore off the pants from his body and held himself up right above her.

"Fuck me," she repeated like in a trance. "Fuck..."

Her voice died on her and gave way to a loud moan as he thrust his mighty erection into her. "Oh God," she groaned in pleasure.

Ridden with blind desire, Nicholas had lost control of her thoughts the moment he had gone in her. But he wasn't worried; the only thing he could focus on was to take care of his arousal. Being inside her, pushing in and out of her felt so good.

"He's not here," he responded under his breath. "It's just you and me."

With these words his pelvis pushed against her more forcefully, driving his hardness deeper into her.

"More," she pleaded. "Please, do me harder." "As you wish."

With several abrupt flaps of his wings, he let go of her and rose into the air. "Turn around," he ordered firmly.

"As soon as she obeyed and presented him with her well-shaped butt, he lunged at her with one powerful flap of his wings, penetrating deeply from behind, making her yell in pleasure. His big claws cupped her full breasts while he kept pushing his hard member inside her, over and over again. She spread her legs wider so he could reach her deeper, and joined the intense, fast rhythm in which Nicholas was doing her.

His long tail bent forward between her thighs and started to rub her, heightening the pleasure he was already giving her with his erection.

She gave a heavy groan. "You're making me come!"

Interpreting this as a plea to increase pressure, he pushed his tail harder against her sweet spot, moving it back and forth. Her hips were responding in faster thrusts, maximizing her sexual pleasure until she yelled.

Her entire body stiffened and shivered heavily/ "Oh God, I'm coming, oh God!"

At this moment Nicholas thrust one more time into her as deeply as he could, and with an otherworldly growl, he released all his sexual tension of the past few days into her.

CHAPTER 4

SWEET ITALIAN MEAT

YOU HAVE PROBABLY HEARD the old saying that Italian dudes have big cocks, haven't you? Well, guess what? In my case, this seems to be the absolute truth. I had always been hung like a horse for as long as I could remember. My dad and brothers are all huge too.

Let me just say we have no trouble finding hot dates.

My issue was that I was tired of the boring little wimpy dates I was having these days. My nine, nearly nine and a half, inch dick needed more of a woman than I had been screwing lately. I seemed to end up with one of two kinds of girls. They were either Italians like me with big hair and even worse attitudes and absolutely boring as fuck in the sack or white girls who wanted to lay there like they were dead and make me do all of the work and bang their cunts until they were sore.

I decided it was time for me to step out of my comfort zone a bit. I wanted to fuck a woman as if I had never had the privilege of sticking my Italian meat in before. My dad owned an Italian eatery and he had a black girl that worked for him who was so hot she gave me instant wood. I had always wanted a black girl and wondered what their pink pussies were like on the inside. I loved how the pink stood out so starkly from the black outer folds. I couldn't wait to dive into one. I went to see this chick at the restaurant that night making sure I looked my very best and that I wore pants that accentuated my huge bulge for her.

I knew she also had a crush on me. I had plans on reeling her in the rest of the way tonight. I also had plans of fucking her brains out. She had a hot body that practically begged to be screwed hard and fast and then excruciatingly slow almost to the point of being painful. I enjoyed a bit of psychological pain involved in my sex and I knew that made me sound like a sexual deviant but I had learned to accept that part of me. It was the inner beast within and I couldn't wait to unleash it.

SEDUCING MY EBONY LOVER

Brittany and I went on and on talking for a few hours comparing people we knew on the internet. I noticed her glimpsing down at my crotch a few times. It didn't take long before we were all out flirting with one another and trying to get away from there. As soon as we got a quiet table in the back, we started to play with each other's crotches.

Our breaths quickly turned to fevered sighs of erotic thrills.

When my dad headed to the kitchen, Brittany and I high-tailed it out the door to my car parked outside. Once inside the erotic vehicle, we attacked each other's mouths with no hint of being held back. We were both very horny people and I couldn't wait for her pussy. Before I fucked her black snatch for the ride of my Italian cock's life, I slowly made my way down between her legs. I buried my entire face within her folds and I swear her snatch held on for dear life. She writhed upon my tongue as my mouth played her like an instrument.

She arched her gorgeous chocolate hips towards me and pressed so hard into me that it took my breath away. I didn't mind though. She tasted of honey and sweet cream and when I raised my head from within her tunnel, I had white pussy cream on my chin and I could smell her potent elixir all over the car. She was now practically begging me to fuck her brains out. I couldn't resist her as she feverishly whined like a puppy to be screwed hard.

I first mounted her nubile body and inched myself between her lovely dark thighs. She moaned in sweet ecstasy, as my Italian sausage grew bigger around as it inched itself deep into her starving cunt. I could feel him swell like a bulbous and throbbing sore muscle dying to be relieved. I screwed her for a while this way and then she mounted me with her big nasty wet pussy. Damn it felt good to be drenched with the warmest pussy juices I had ever had bathing my dick down like a shower of white froth. Her tits jiggled right in my face as she bounced up and down on my meat. It was a vision of pure paradise seeing her tits lively and full with her nipples protruding.

Fucking Brittany was like a day at the amusement park and I was the only one allowed inside the gates. She was like riding a rollercoaster and the wet log ride all rolled into one delicious treat. I couldn't get enough of her. If she was candy, I'd eat her until I got so sick I had to lie down before digging in again. Yes, she was that tasty and then some!

I could snack on her cunt and fuck her all day and all night if she would let me. She was the best pussy this Italian stallion had ever had. After screwing her so hard, she was breathless and screaming, she latched onto my dick with her mouth and wouldn't let go. She knew her way around a cock that's for sure. Her mouth felt like blankets of sheer elegance wrapped around my throbbing cock shaft and head. I knew it was only momentarily and I was going to shoot off straight down her needy throat. I was right because before too long I was grabbing her head and grinding her deep into my crotch daring her to try and let go.

I refused to let her loosen her mouth vice grip on my cock until every drop of my seed was in her throat and belly. I groaned for a good two minutes like starving horny beats and I came at least 6 wads down Brittany's beautiful mouth nestled between her cherry lips.

CHAPTER 5

LISTENING TO HER CUM

SEVERAL SILVER-CHROMED ELECTRODES were stuck all over my bloated throbbing cock. A sexy woman who looked like a Czech Sex Cam girl moved quickly on stage adjusting the projector. She called herself Anna. She was too beautiful and too stylish in her pearl drop silver earrings. I wanted to propose to the cutie not help her run her "Men and Sex Papers Experiment."

Anna's flawless makeup accentuated her narrow eyes. Anna pushed buttons and adjusted the camera as it came on the big picture screen. Her beautiful face and brunette shag hairdo went on the screen and collectively all of us men sighed in frustration.

"Oh Czech Anna," I muttered.

She addressed us from the stage, "This experiment is to measure your reaction to women's sexual excitement. Press the red button if you think the woman came or is coming. Press the blue button if you think she has not come."

How she managed to give those hot-ass instructions without blushing baffled me. My dick throbbed an 8.0 on the scale every time she said come. Which I visualized as "C-U-M."

All I thought about was Czech Ann smiling, drinking my jism like it was white wine, licking the head of my cock it was a lollipop. She came around to each of us and didn't smile at many. To one guy, she flashed a bored facial expression. Another got a frown. Her frown made me think of sex, too. See, Czech Anna, with her professionally cut brunette shag hairstyle, wrapped blinders around our eyes! We had to listen to the videos of the women's sexual moans, gasps, giggles, laughs, guffaws, chortles, snickers, squeals, and silent breathing--then press a button telling if the woman came or not. For that frown to be the last thing seen before hearing women's sexual verbal responses would be a sad thing indeed.

Each of us pre-pushed our pants below our knees. Each had huge a fluffy white towel to catch any...say effusions of enthusiasm for the women's voices.

As Anna came around to me, her face changed from neutral to a slight knowing look of "Oh you're big," as I stroked my hot pink dick up and down. "Anna you're really from Czechoslovakia, right?"

A surprised shot on her face, "Why yes," Her eyelids had lowered and the smoke brown-bronze makeup below her eyebrows turned her sexual curiosity into lustful anticipation. The flat bridge of her short nose shined like a lighthouse drawing your attention to the narrow space between her lovely brown eyes. Normally such narrow eyes make her look ugly or goofy. But those Czech girls always have something that should not work visually on their faces that turns them into sex goddesses. Then and there, I wanted to feel Czech Anna's pretty round tip nose brush against the dark curly brunette groin hairs of thrusting hips, My cock sinking deep down her gullet.

"Czech girls are the most beautiful in the world." I managed to say nonchalantly.

"For me, Czech girls are the most beautiful." She touched me more than usual as she made sure each chrome probe fitted to the right blood veins on my cock.

"See we must measure exactly the blood flow," she added.

One probe rested on the underside of my hard column of flesh on the major blood highway. She had placed another one on the underside of my cockhead. These probes were flexible as a durable foil. Jerking off was not only allowed but encouraged.

"We need to see if you're more accurate in predicting a woman's sexual state as your own sexual state rises," She said this experiment would help the genders to meet in the center. She gave my huge dick a purring pat. I thought the experiment focused on gravity and antigravity. My cock kept trying to stay up, but eventually, the leap upward resulted in the downward falling action.

Anna went on to the next guy. After five minutes, I smelt the musky whiff of pussy under my nose.

"That's to make sure you get the highest score," Czech Anna said. "We can then continue this experiment's second phase in a private office."

Her pussy smelled like a flower garden on a rainy day. I imagined her opened pussy flowering before my long thin fingers, slipping between her cunt folds, manipulating the excited sex feelings of Anna's overheating pussy.

We listen to one girl, then another. Some girls clearly were dressed outside somewhere on a park bench. Others were inside a room by themselves laughing on the phone. Finally, I got the hang of it. I started pressing the red and blue buttons. I believe Anna's sex scent put me in a more positive mood. I was less cautious. I became more attentive to the nuances of the women's pants and groans.

The girl's frustrated sexual auditory expression made me sexually frustrated, too. When the girls came, I came mentally. I held off long as possible. One Chinese girl made so much noise coming that I pressed the red button before she finished coming after moaning for ten minutes. I got the surprise of my life when I heard a familiar giggle beside the lone sound of a fish tank burbling in the background. That was Anna plunging her fingers into her pussy. Her squish

squish sound counteracted the fish tank, her pacing the same as when she talked to me. Somehow, all my senses put it all together and an even stronger whiff of her musky-flower cunt overtook my senses as I came. I came. I was shot for the rest of the experiment. At least the white towel caught all my cum.

I pressed the red and blue buttons the best I could.

So it surprised me when I received a call from Czech Anna. "You scored the highest in the experiment. I'll be waiting for you in my office. Friday afternoon at three o'clock."

"That was you and the fish tank." "You'll find out when arrive. Do hurry!"

I took a shower and bought a bouquet of roses. And made my way to her office on campus. When she opened the locked door, I immediately heard the fish tank, burbling in the background. Anna smiled. She took the flowers as I walked past her. "Make yourself comfortable."

I took off my shirt and pants and sat on the black couch by the fish tank. "I'm ready Anna."

Anna returned and put the flowers in a vase on the table in front of the couch. "I can see." She reached out and stroked my hard pink cock.

Anna taught me other ways to understand women's sexual responses. I'm a much better man for it, believe me!

CHAPTER 6

MAID TO ORDER

I AM a chambermaid at a major hotel chain. I must say my job gets pretty dull at times. I go in, clean, layout fresh towels and soaps and then I'm onto the next room. I was starting my typical rounds from rooms 15 to 35 this particular morning when I came upon the hottest patron I had ever seen in my life.

I used my card and entered room 22 ready to clean my little heart out when I noticed a man was in the shower. I hollered out to alert him I was the maid there to clean. He yelled back a quick "okay" so I went about my business. I was making his bed and cleaning up around his bedside table when I noticed he had some dirty magazines I did a quick giggle and went about my duties. I moved on to vacuuming and had my back turned so I didn't see the nude man emerge from the shower until I felt someone poke me on the shoulder. I jumped and turned around to see a sight that totally caught me off guard but pleased my eyes too.

There stood my patron in his birthday suit. He had quite an impressive birthday suit too, I might add. He had a tall muscular frame that showed signs of him visiting a gym or weight room quite often. His muscles still beaded with water from his shower rippled with the droplets. I made my way down past his six-pack abs to a boner that was at least 8 inches in length and big around in girth as well. I couldn't help but say "mmmmm" when I saw it. He was obviously turned on and it stood straight out like a steel rod. He grabbed his cock and began to stroke up and down the smooth shaft with very smooth and determined strokes. It made my pussy absolutely wet with need.

He took my willing right hand and guided it to his throbbing muscle. I didn't resist and I took over the stroking action for him. We hardly spoke a word as I pulled up and down on his hard-on. He then said a few words and asked me if I'd like to taste it. I nodded yes, and then dropped to my knees. I looked up and could see him watching me suck him in the mirror that was right beside him attached to the dresser. It made me even hotter to know he was watching me give him a blow job. My hand by habit made its way down to my horny snatch. I stuck two fingers inside it and started to finger myself hard.

He seemed to approve and looked down at my hand moving in and out of my cunt ferociously. He pushed my head down harder onto his throbbing girth. It wasn't long before he and I headed to the just-made bed. I admit my pussy wanted his dick inside of it in the worst way. I was so horny I could hardly contain my excitement. I had always fantasized about this very scenario happening in one of the rooms I was cleaning. I was in shock that my fantasy was coming true right before my very eyes. The fact that this was a favorite dream of mine made it even hotter and more erotic.

Before he fucked me he went down on me. He ate my pussy like a pro. I had never eaten this good in my life. He first kissed my inner thighs gently and seductively. It made me quiver with anticipation. I propped myself up on my elbows so I could see his mouth and tongue do their magic on my greedy cunt. He lapped at my lips and sucked my rock-hard clit right up until the point I was ready to cum and he backed off. It felt so good having strange sex. It added to the eroticism of the whole experience. He ate me out for a while and then I grabbed his hands and pulled him up to me indicating to him that I was ready to have my brains fucked out. He willingly complied. You could smell the scent of sex fill the room. I could see the animal desire in his eyes as he guided his rock-hard dick inside.

He placed both of my long legs up around his shoulders and started thrusting in and out of me. He would inch his cock inside me a few inches at a time and then pull out. It teased my drenched pussy, and only made me desire to be fucked more and more. I could hardly take the teasing but it felt good all at the same time. He flipped me over and started to fuck me in the same manner. He guided his cock in a few inches at a time practically making my pussy scream with greedy need. I moaned loudly like an animal in heat filled with lusty desire. I pounded my ass backward toward his cock begging for the whole length of it at once. Just when I thought he may deprive me of ever feeling the entire 8 inches in me he thrust it in with full force. It hurt and felt amazing all at the same time. He slammed hard into my ass and I could feel his cum filled balls slapping my ass cheeks and underneath them.

He grabbed my jiggling ass while he fucked me digging his fingernails into my flesh. The raw lust was incredibly invigorating and only added to the heated desire for sex the two of us shared. I knew it wasn't long before he released a long stream of white-hot cum deep within my cunt. I could feel his balls grow tighter and tighter with each thrust of his needy dick. Then suddenly his rod stood erect as steel. I could feel it in my pussy and he released his cum. He groaned out loud and tensed his entire body and I could almost feel the hot flow inside as it shot out of his cock eye.

Shortly thereafter I creamed my cunt all over the length of his shaft. I screamed in pleasure that I am sure the people in the room next door could hear. It was one of the best orgasms I had ever had. Having sex with a complete stranger was as good as or better than I had ever imagined.

After fucking the cock in room 22 I went about my day cleaning with a smile on my face knowing the taboo sex I had just taken part in. That alone was worth the thrill of being a maid to order.

CHAPTER 7

RED: NO STRINGS ATTACHED

FUCK, she was a little hottie. Derek was not one for redheads, most of all women that were white, but damn his preferences went out the door when she walked into the club in her black leather mini and silver sequined tie top. And the black thigh-high leather boots that she wore were kick ass. He could tell that this one was going to be the one that made him go for a white girl no matter how much his boys or family did not like it.

Throughout the night, he could not take his eyes off of her. He loved how she moved so fluidly on the dance floor and he had to admit he was impressed when she knew how to step. He could swear that she was black herself, and the way that her breasts bounced as she moved was what drove him crazy the most.

Just then one of his buddies came up behind him "Hey man, we are going over to Dyondre's, are you down bro?"

" Naw, Ty, I am going to stay here tonight. I am going to take someone home tonight if you know what I mean?" Derek grinned mischievously.

"Alright man, I will see you tomorrow. Peace out"

Derek knew that with Ty gone, we could do anything he wanted and he was not going to criticize him or tell him how a white girl like Red would be nothing but trouble. But hey, he knew what he had to have and she was the one he wanted and that was all there was to it.

Gathering himself, he made his way over to her. Damn, she even smelled good. As he made his way dancing, she actually came up to him, grinding against him and wrapping her one arm around his neck. Fuck, she was good and it was so hard to not get an erection right there in front of everyone. As they continued to dance, he could not help himself from wrapping his arm around her waist. He wanted to show her what he felt with her dancing with him.

As he began grinding up against she bent over and started to undulate her body more, making him harder by the time that the song was done he was so hard it hurt to walk anywhere. "Hey, red can I buy you a drink? I mean, that is the least I could do for you."

Walking with Derek, she smiled. "Do you know what you can do for me? How about you and I go to the back and fuck? I mean, I know when I saw you that you were staring at me, and I have to say you are not at all bad yourself tiger." Damn that was fast, he thought. He was not used to women being so upfront and honest. But he was not going to let that stop him he would take her up on her offer.

She took ahold of his hand and led him to the back room. She knew that the back room was meant for private lap dances and other erotic interludes. So she thought she would take it on herself to lock the room so that they would not get interrupted. Making sure that no one would bother her, she shut off her cell phone.

Derek sat in a chair as she began to dance in front of him while slowly taking off of her top. Damn her body was impeccable and her breasts are bigger than he thought. As she finished getting undressed, he quickly took off his white tank top showing his muscular chest. Then he stood up taking his pants off.

Just as he was about to come up behind her, she turned facing him.

Picking her up he put her back up against the wall and she automatically wrapped her long legs around his waist as he began to thrust his large cock into her tight throbbing pussy. God, he could bang her all night long. But there was something that really set red aside from the usual women that he liked to fuck and that was the fact that she was the type to get right down to busy and she did not waste any time playing with him. She was real. As he continued to make love to her, he could hear her moaning the deeper that he would delve in to her

"Oh yeah, come on baby harder, pound it harder into me"

Derek could not help it, he loved the way that sounded. And he had to admit he loved how she had accepted him with him being black. Lifting her up in the air and standing her up in front of him. Bending her over he began to take her again.

"That's it baby arch for me."

As she began to arch Derek wrapped his hands in her long red hair and she did something that he did not think she would. She began picking up the pace faster to the point he thought he was going to explode. Fuck, he wanted to keep going but he knew that if he did he was going to end up losing himself and he did not want that. Pulling his cock out he turned her around and she got on her knees, taking his cock into her mouth. Damn, she was good she knew what exactly to do to get him off. He could not wish for anything more when it came to women. Derek was sure that after tonight he definitely would not be the same with any women. Red would be the one that he would remember from this night on. As he exploded in her mouth she looked up with the most sensual look on her face, he could tell that she was definitely sexually sated and it was going to be the best night for her as well, and the best part is there is no strings attached which was the way they both wanted it.

CHAPTER 8

RUTTING FOR LIFE

I WALKED in on my girlfriend, Italia. She is a hot platinum blonde with beach-curled hair and a European sense of fashion. I love the girl more than I should. I can't dump her because she always surprises me. I like surprises. Her surprises turned me into her groupie. One time I came home and she tied herself up in cellophane. She wrapped every place on her hot body except her pussy, asshole, and mouth.

"You can fuck me any place I'm not wrapped up," she panted breathlessly.

Another time, I woke up and found myself covered in whip cream. She said, "You can't go to work until I've finished licking you clean." I had a hard time explaining that one to my boss.

Now I couldn't help laughing, "You . . . a lezzie!" I watched the cool, cynical expression on the woman's face. She wore a black corset and lace thigh-high stockings, a garter belt on her spread legs. Her legs were spread in the shape of a diamond. Her thick tuft of black pubic hair was wet, barely hiding her thick clitoris. Italia had her forefinger and index finger spreading the beautiful babe's glistening inner labia lips. The raven-haired cutie lay back on my bed mushing together her modest tits sticking two inches out from her rib cage.

"It's not what you think, HoneyBear," Italia said, after rising and showing her gorgeous face. Her face shined in a coating of female girly goo. She rose and kissed me on the lips. She hugged me and pulled me down on the bed sitting beside her friend. After Italia stopped pushing the girl's sweet musky pussy scent all down my throat, she stopped and introduced us. "Troy, this is Tracey."

I rubbed Tracey's inner thighs. Her copious amount of girl sauce made a big wet spot on the bed. "I'm glad to meet you, Tracey."

"HoneyBear, it's not what you think," she warned me again.

"I want to enjoy some Tracey, too," I said to Italia. That's when I heard a growl.

My hand sensed a thick strand of fur. In a second, the girl turned on her hips and transformed from a pretty woman into a German shepherd size wolf, her teeth growling and frowning at me.

I jumped up.

. . .

"I told you it's not what you think, HoneyBear!" She got up and slipped on her black tutu and bra. "Come here, Tracey." Italia cooed. "He didn't mean any harm." She bent down and held the muzzle of the big hot pink wolf in her hands. She patted her and soothed her thick furry coat. The wolf's dark eyes glared at me. I pulled back and buttoned up my pants.

"She's a fucking wolf!"

"She's a werewolf, not a real wolf, HoneyBear." Italia straddled the wolf and forced it to sit down. The She-Wolf panted and her eyes seemed lighter, less menacing.

"Long as you have control over her." I got up to go into the bathroom to jack off. I couldn't forget about the beautiful sight I'd seen. Her pussy scent still coated my face. I wanted to fuck. "I'll just be in the bathroom, jacking off."

After I went into the bathroom, pulled down my pants, and peed, I was about to jack off when Italia came into the bathroom. She bent over the tub. "You can fuck me HoneyBear! You're a good husband."

I smiled wide. "I've been burning to fuck you since noon." Italia replied, "I like it when your voice has a manly growl to it."

· · ·

I slipped inside Italia, and my dick hit that sweet spot inside her and she let out a low snarl of her own. That is when I remember it, Italia hadn't locked the bathroom door! I heard a vicious growl and there she was again. That huge She-wolf.

"She keeps growing."

"She can change to any size she wants." My hard-on started dwindling.

"No No No! Fuck me HoneyBear!" Italian begged. "Once she sees we're good for one another, she won't be jealous.

My voice shook a bit, but I kept fucking. Aahhhhhhh...I was about to come when I felt these two soft warm hands slip over my black shoulders and cup my pectoral muscles. Those hands pinched my nipples and I felt a hot wet tongue lick the salt off my black neck. Then I felt long legs strad-dling mine. I slowed down, still humping Italia, and saw her lace black stocking legs beside my own. Her wet pussy squished against my lower back. I felt good.

"See. . . Tracey likes you too."

"I can't hold back." I blasted down the little space inside Italia's young cunt. Then as I slipped out, I felt Tracey's hands slide down to my softening cock.

"Tracey has magic saliva."

"Magic saliva?" I soon realized it didn't matter if I came once, Tracey's saliva went around my cock, and blood flowed strong and hard back into my dickhead.

. . .

Tracey nudged-pushed Italia out of the way.

Italia said, "She wants to see if you can mate with her."
"I'd be glad to."

"You mate with a wolf; you mate for life!"

"That's fine with me." I started fucking and Tracey stood very still. So still, I wondered if she was enjoying it at all. Then finally, she started humping back, following my rhythm. At last, we got into a frothy good rutting pace. Ten minutes. Fifteen minutes. Seventeen minutes and I slipped my hands under her belly and massaged her tits. Her tits were twice as big as my girlfriend's and she's got DD tits. "Hey, she can change her body to any shape."

"Yep," Italia said, using her slutty voice. "She likes you. You're hooked up now." "Hooked up?"

"Yeah," Italia waited until I tried to disengage. "Hey, I can't seem to pull out!"

A low growl sounded before me. "You're not through coming." "Yeah, I am."

Tracey turned back and her face seemed narrow like a She-wolf again for a second. Then it seemed normal.

Italian giggled. "Not until she says your finished coming."

Tracey started humping back and I didn't shrink. So I sighed and kept fucking. Italia went to the kitchen and brought back a bottle of white wine.

. . .

"Take a sip, HoneyBear, this is going to take a while." She raised the goblet to my lips and I drank it.

She handed a goblet to Tracey bent over the bathtub and she drank, too.

We fucked like that for at least two hours straight before I finally came enough times to disengage.

"I guess we're a threesome now," Tracey said and offered Italia a soft She-Wolf lick. "Seems so."

"I'm up for you, again," I swaggered my black cock around. "Italia, you want to do the honors?" Italia briefly changed into a She-Wolf and snarled. Then she changed back into her human self. "I thought you'd never catch on, Troy."

"Italia, you know too much about She-Wolves to be a mere human babe."

CHAPTER 9

THE PERFECT DESSERT

WE LIKE TO PLAY GAMES. Play them until she begs me for it, pleads for it. But even then, I continue to tease her. I am never satisfied. Not until her ass is up and her face down; preferably on the dirty floor. Never satisfied until she becomes utterly silent and just waits for me to ram her, her pussy gleaming in whatever lighting I had set up, be it candles or a gentle night-lamp. But even then, the candles are just a tease, a game. Sometimes they even end up being something to put in her ass while I fuck her from behind.

As usual, it is I who begins the evening's entertainment. Start it with a perfectly ordinary, perfectly boring dinner. It is romantic, to be sure, but I know this isn't what she really wants. Candles and music are but the ambiance, a lube of sorts – a prelude. She wants something her husband could never give her. She wants domination and a cock as hard as the wood of the chair she sits on.

I cook for her and use only the freshest ingredients and spices to entice her with all manner of pleasant scents. We barely finish our meal, when I look into her eyes and lick my lips, smile a most mischievous smile, and say, "I have a present for you." There are no delusions about the nature of my gift.

She looks excited, but I know she hopes I would just grab her. But not quite yet. Not until I see every bit of that wine she had drunk run down between her legs. I stand up and pull out a black blindfold made of the smoothest material. It might have been silk, or it might have been something that fools girls like her that I care about anything else but fucking the shit out of them. But being gentle is easy. Especially when I know she wants the opposite. I place it over her eyes. I pull down my pants and watch her breathing quicken as I grab her hand and coil her fingers around my stiff cock. It's so thick her fingers don't even meet. She grabs it with both hands and begins to suck on it. Her lips are something that follows and finds you in your dreams and makes you cum. But a taste is enough, I pull her back by the hair and whisper, "Not yet, princess, get on your knees." I help her along, just in case she gets any ideas about not doing exactly what I want.

She obeys without a word, knows we're playing our game now, my game. I place her hands on my thighs and open her mouth with my hand, gently, stopping inches before her lips so she could smell it and feel the heat radiating from it. She sticks out her tongue and licks it, flinches as I slap her with my dick

"No, you don't. You know better," I say.

She begs me to do it again, but instead, I waited for a while, waited, waited, and smiled. Instead of my dick, I spit on her face and slap her with my hand, then ram it in her mouth. I watch and hear as she utterly enjoys it and pleads with me not to stop. But I do. I replace my fingers with my cock and ram her head on it. I had expected the opposite than her grabbing my ass and helping me fuck her mouth.

The sounds she makes make my cock even harder. When she loses control and begins to use her teeth, I slap her with my dick still in her mouth. Tears run down her face, smudging her make-up. The bitch bit me. I stop only to get her on her feet, turn her around, place her over the table and tear off the dress I had bought her a day earlier.

"You're going be a good little slut tonight. Otherwise, I'll have to leave you naked outside my door. I'm going to do anything I want with you, and you're going to do everything I want."

I slap her ass and rub it, spit on it, make it shine, squeezed it, then slap hard enough to leave an imprint on it. Her ass is unusually huge for her waist, shaking with each subsequent slap, the sound of it echoing. She truly is something you'd want to fuck until your dick bleeds. She yelps and arches her back with each of my hits, the sweat gleaming on her. She tries to stop me, but I grab both of her arms, grip them behind her, and observe her for a few moments as her breathing quickens even further. She knew what came next. Yet I keep her waiting a while longer. I slam my whole fucker inside her in one thrust. She cries out with pleasure, comes, and then comes again while I filled her up time and time again. I feel her juices dripping as her thighs shake with a fresh orgasm.

"Come in my mouth, daddy. Please!" But if there's one thing I don't respond to, it's begging. And the bitch knew better. She wanted me to come in her mouth, fair enough, a request I was all too happy to oblige. But not yet. Her ass comes first. I turn her on her back, my fingers wet with her juices as I fuck her asshole with it. I could smell the fragrance of her pussy, the heat of it, as I lick her, ear her like her clit was the last thing I'd ever eat. I run my whole tongue over it, spit on it, the mix of saliva and pussy juice running from her lips to my tongue, I slap it and fill it up one finger at a time, until three of them nest inside. I remove the last from her ass and replace it with my thick cock. I do it slowly, all the way. She cannot utter a sound as it slowly goes in and out. In and out. Like fucking clockwork. When she regains a bit of herself, all she can manage is a faint, "Oh god, oh god, oh god..."

I slowly jam more of my fingers into her pussy and, in synchronized motions, fucked both of her holes. She opened up like a fountain, spilling her wetness all over my chest, the smell of it like some nectar the gods drink at their tables to quench their hungry cocks.

She had made herself ready for my full fist. If she had been quiet before, she was utterly silent now as I fill her up completely. I don't even have to say it as I pound her, my stomach ramming my hand deeper into her pussy. I didn't even have to tell her to spread her legs. She did it all by herself

"Good girl." I grab her by the throat and fuck her like I know she hadn't been fucked before, her face tells me as much. She begins to shake and twist, a sound like an ultimate release of pleasure escaping her open mouth. I remove her blindfold and pull her to her knees. I want to see her eyes for this. I watch her pant, still in the grip of orgasm, her gaze locked with mine as I spray her mouth and face, see her swallow her perfect dessert.

CHAPTER 10

THE SEDUCTIVE INTERN

I WOKE up Monday morning raring to go to the office where I was beginning my internship with one of the most brilliant, easy-going, and sexiest surgeons at Boston Memorial Hospital. I was so excited to be finally getting some hands-on training as a gynecologist with one of the best female physicians in Boston.

I dressed classily yet not too sexily, so as not to give him the impression I was just in the frame of mind to get my cunt rocks off. Although looking at him always did get my pussy drenched and at times looking at his dick pressing through his britches and sometimes even under his white coat got my lips ripe and ready to be sucked. My pussy actually dribbled once just thinking of his bulbous-headed dick slipping inside my snapper.

Today as I made it into the office building, he and I were doing exams of women about ready to have their babies. I got to see him with his hand on a cunt. It drove me nuts thinking of it. I took a side trip to the little girl's room. While in there, I pulled my sensitive brown lips and fingered my bush hair. I got my cunt to near orgasm and had to squeeze my lips around my fingers to stop. It was all I could do not to spray the floor down with cream. But I was able to contain it and I didn't cum. I wanted to save the sweet release for a more sexually exciting adventure.

I met up with Dr. Bassett in the hallway and as instructed, I followed him to an exam room with a very pregnant and beautiful young woman. She was sitting on the edge of the exam tables one of those hideous gowns they insist on making patients wear.

"Linsey Smithson I'd like to introduce my intern, Haley Glenn. "

"Nice to meet you, Linsey," I said and offered my right hand for her to shake which she did.

"Linsey is due in one week," Dr. Glenn said to me, and it made me practically swoon. "So we are going to do an exam to check the baby, dilation and you know the drill." He said smiling sexily at me and nearly melting m. I could tell Linsey felt the same. I know this is naughty but I got lost in the thought of being in her shoes with this man's fingers toying around my very pregnant and horny cunt. I knew from medical training that pregnancy guarantees uncontrollable pussy swelling. It supposedly makes a woman almost cum just grazing her nipples or pussy on anything. I truly had to stop my right middle finger from making its way to my now throbbing and hot pussy.

The doctor and I got Linsey to lie back as we each helped her get a foot in the cold stirrups. I will never forget the next thing. By the time I got down pussy eye view with Dr. Barrett I nearly squirted on myself. Her pussy was so fucking pink and swollen. It was easy for a doctor to tell she was no stranger to fingering and fucking. I would almost guess by the length of her juicy, bulbous pussy lips that our Linsey was no stranger to fucking herself with anything and fingering herself probably 3 times a day. A girl's pussy didn't get hard and huge like this for nothing.

As Dr. Barrett began his examination, you could cut the sexual energy in the room with a scalpel. It was easy to see we were all turned on. He first felt her tits and dribbles of white cream drizzled out of them the bumps on the areola were protruding and her nipples were ripe and ready to suck. I would have loved to have wrapped my brown pussy lips around one of them and then have her eat the milk of my cunt. She was making me so damn horny I could hardly contain my moans of pleasure. I looked down and saw the doc had a boner going on as well. Linsey squirmed her ass on the table obviously holding back an orgasm. Her belly clenched up in a contraction and her lips began to pulse all by themselves.

I was hoping we could witness an orgasm of the grandest kind. She then surprised the doctor and me both, and reached over and grabbed my cunt and stuck her fingers under my skirt. I moaned and humped her hand ferociously. She asked me to eat her giant lips. I took my time with each lip, pulling so slow she began to quiver almost uncontrollably. Dr. Bassett rammed his cock down her throat and she squeezed her puffy nipples so hard milk dripped down her tummy all the way to her raging cunt. I got a taste of sweet milk as I ravaged her delicious fat cunt lips. Her cunt lips were like mine only stiffer and her lips formed the hood making them just puffy enough to yank and pull on ferociously. Her cunt would not let me stop consuming every inch of it. Her lips literally splayed against my cheeks like two butterfly wings. She was jerking her butt up and down by now her belly a rigid orgasmic contraction.

She started the process of orgasm and we thought she might never let up. The doctor and I watched both wanking off and he taking one nipple in his mouth and me the other as her tits gushed milk everywhere. Then her cunt began to spray cream straight up into the air drenching us all three. She actually hit herself in the face with the powerful gush acting like a rabid animal licking and lapping it up. Finally, Linsey slowed down her contractions as we saw her tummy relax from its rigid form. The whole time she plunged her fist in and out of her huge cunt with lips wrapped tightly around her wrist. She yanked her fist out and gushed on the table as it dripped to the floor I dropped to my knees catching the drips upon my tongue and the doctor sprayed cock cream all over my face.

Needless to say, this was one of the most exciting exams the doctor and I did all day, and I could only hope to be there when Linsey gave birth to assist her in any need she might have.

ABOUT THE AUTHOR

Helana Parkins is an emerging erotica author of many erotica kinks and sub-genres. Be sure to check out other books and leave a review if this story got you hot!

Visit my blog at Helana Parkins Blog

Join my newsletter for exclusive previews Helana Parkins Newsletter

Sign up for Free Stories from Xplicit Press Authors

Xplicit Press Author Updates

Like Xplicit Press on Facebook

Follow Xplicit Press on Twitter

Readers: I want to expand a few of the stories to see where the characters can be explored further. If there are any of the stories that you would like to read more about again, I'd love to hear from you!

Keep In Touch
Helana Parkins
info@helanaparkins.com